To Janet and Sam –
who know what this is all about. With love, Tom

For Yuta and Kenta and all their teeth! L.C.

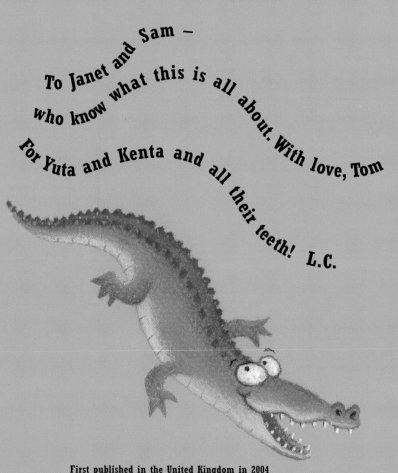

First published in the United Kingdom in 2004
by Chrysalis Children's Books, an imprint of Chrysalis Books Group
The Chrysalis Building
Bramley Road
London W10 6SP
www.chrysalisbooks.co.uk
This edition distributed by Publishers Group West

Designed by Sarah Goodwin and Keren-Orr Greenfeld

BRITISH LIBRARY CATALOGUING-IN-PUBLICATION DATA
A catalogue record for this book is available from the British Library

ISBN 1 84458 241 8

Printed in Hong Kong.

OPEN WIDE!

Tom Barber
Illustrated by Lynne Chapman

Chrysalis Children's Books

Sam did not like going to the dentist, not one little bit. Yes, the waiting room had a fish tank and he got a sticker and a treat from Dad afterward, but that was not nearly enough to make it all right.

"Good morning, Sam," said Dr. Murgatroyd, the dentist.
Sam looked at the bright light overhead...
the funny chair that looked like it
might close on you with a snap...
and the tray of pointy metal
things on the little table.

Sam felt Dad let go of his arm. Now was his chance. Sam made a dash for it...

"Come out this second, Sam," said Dad.
"No," growled Sam.

"Leave it to me, Mr. Spurr," said Dr. Murgatroyd. And before Sam knew what was happening, the dentist had squeezed under the chair with him.

"You know, Sam, you'd be amazed at some of the teeth I have to look at."

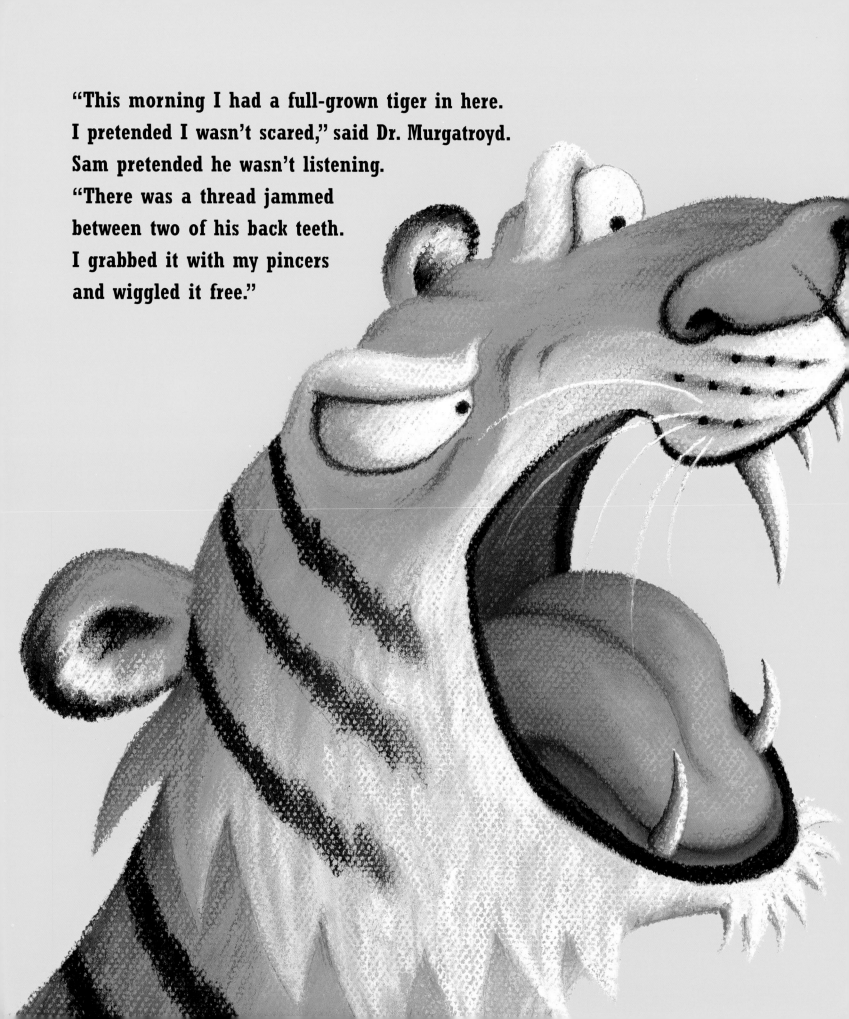

"This morning I had a full-grown tiger in here. I pretended I wasn't scared," said Dr. Murgatroyd. Sam pretended he wasn't listening. "There was a thread jammed between two of his back teeth. I grabbed it with my pincers and wiggled it free."

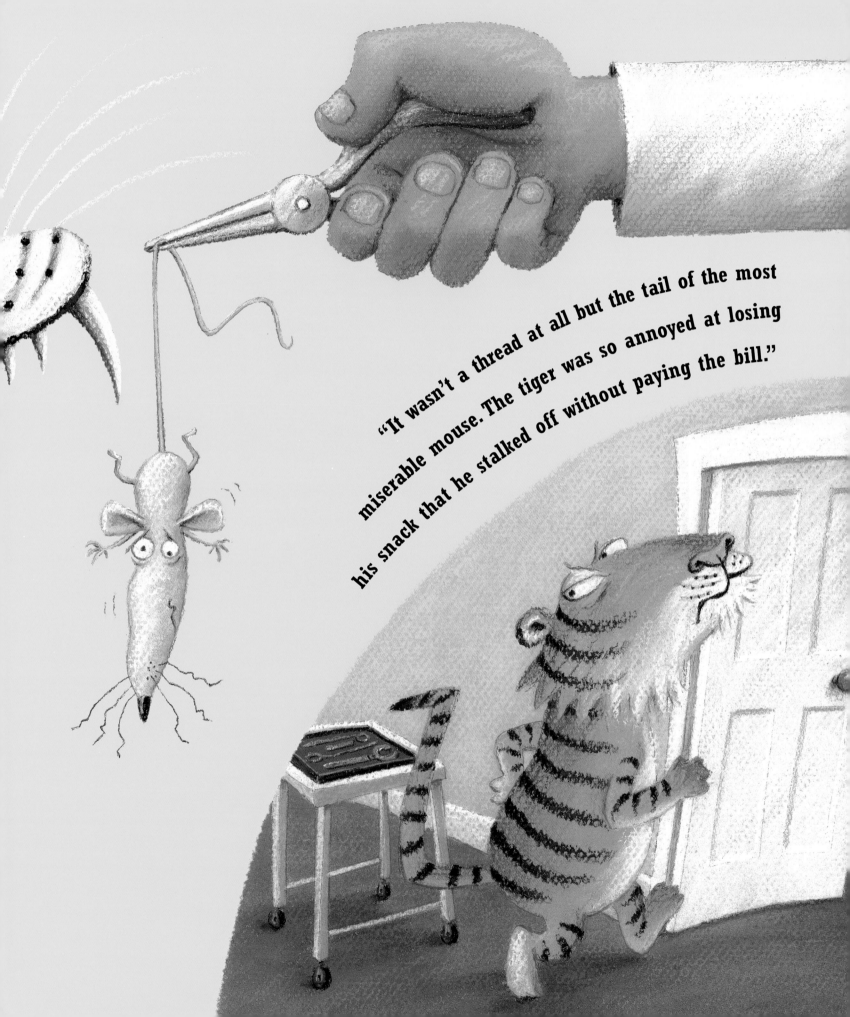

"It wasn't a thread at all but the tail of the most miserable mouse. The tiger was so annoyed at losing his snack that he stalked off without paying the bill."

"And that's not all," continued Dr. Murgatroyd. "See that hole there? An old nanny goat did that. Goats will chew anything and she had already worn out eight pairs of false teeth."

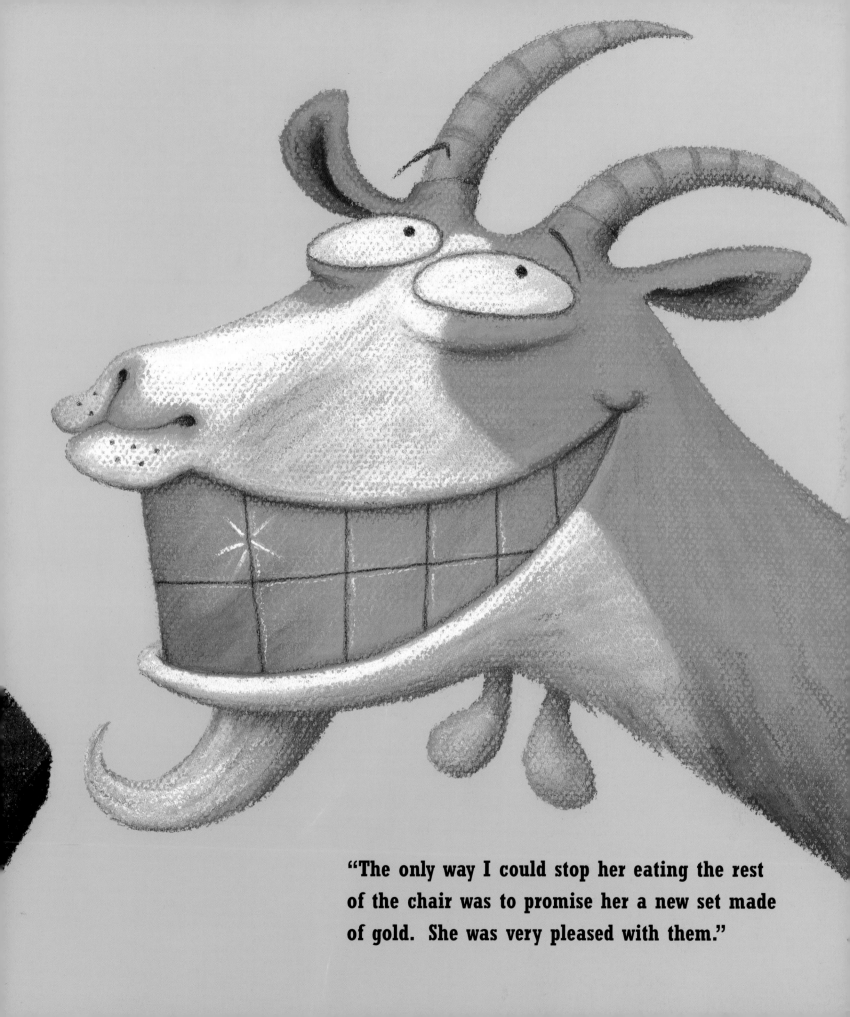

"The only way I could stop her eating the rest of the chair was to promise her a new set made of gold. She was very pleased with them."

"And the week before that, you'll never believe it—a hippo with a toothache! He was even more grumpy than usual. What a massive mouth! I could have climbed right inside."

"One of his front teeth had a big crack in it. It had to come out, of course. I told him he must stop biting boats, but I bet he won't take my advice."

"Do you want to see the tooth?" Sam nodded.

"The Thursday before that we had a visit from a beaver."
"Blunt teeth?" asked Sam, who knew a thing or two about animals.
"How did you guess?" asked Dr. Murgatroyd. "I gave them a good
sharpening with the tooth file. He was very grateful, but he did
insist on trying them out before he left."

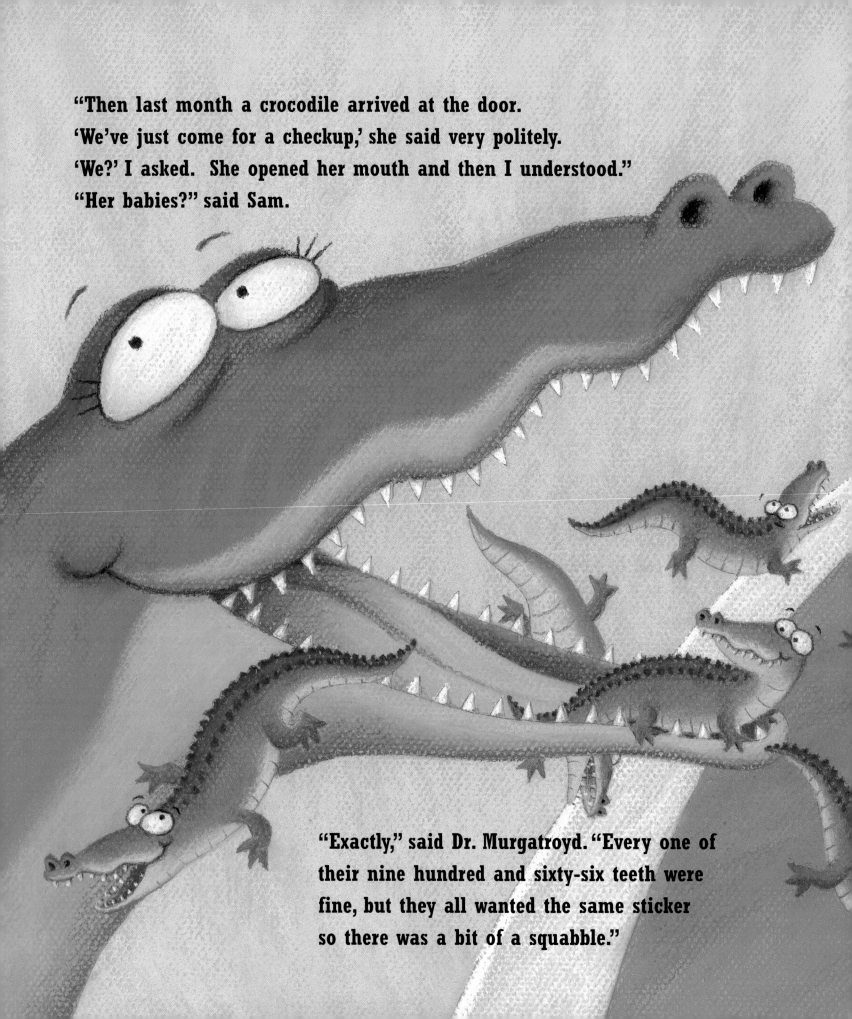

"Then last month a crocodile arrived at the door.
'We've just come for a checkup,' she said very politely.
'We?' I asked. She opened her mouth and then I understood."
"Her babies?" said Sam.

"Exactly," said Dr. Murgatroyd. "Every one of
their nine hundred and sixty-six teeth were
fine, but they all wanted the same sticker
so there was a bit of a squabble."

"Do you want to choose your sticker now?"

"Yes, please," said Sam.

"Take two if you like."

He took three, but Dr. Murgatroyd didn't seem to notice.

"Who else?" asked Sam.

"Well now, I don't normally do beaks, but I couldn't refuse a poor toucan. She had eaten too many overripe mangoes and flown smack into a tree trunk. A twist with the pincers, a splint, and a bandage and that was that."

"If you come and sit in the chair you can see the feathers she gave me," Dr. Murgatroyd said. "They're beautiful," said Sam, "and look, she's laid an egg up there as well."

"What's the biggest animal you've ever looked at?" said Sam. "A humpback whale," said Dr. Murgatroyd. "He had been attacked by a pack of hammerhead sharks. They had smashed big holes in his teeth so he couldn't eat properly. It was quite a job. I bent so many of my tools fixing them I had to buy some new ones. Shall I show you?"

"And what about the scariest?" asked Sam, when he could move his mouth again. "That would have to be the spitting cobra," said Dr. Murgatroyd.

"He's so deadly poisonous, I had to wear chainmail gloves just in case he bit me by mistake. And when it was time for him to rinse and spit in the basin we all had to leave the room."

"You can have a rinse now, Sam. Pink or blue water?" "Blue please," said Sam.

"What with tigers, goats, hippopotamuses, crocodiles, beavers, toucans, whales, and cobras, you're the best patient I've had in that chair for weeks, Sam. Off you go, we're all finished."

"Already? Can I keep the hippo's tooth?" asked Sam.

"Only if you promise to bring it back with you next time you come."

"I will," said Sam, and he showed it to Dad on the way out.

"I didn't believe any of those stories, did you?" said Sam.

"No, of course not," said Dad. "Though I'm not sure where that hippo's tooth came from... Now, are you ready for the monster movie?